Famous Illustrated Tales
PANCHATANTRA
WISDOM STORIES

Maple Kids

Famous Illustrated Tales of
PANCHATANTRA WISDOM STORIES

Published by

MAPLE PRESS PRIVATE LIMITED

Corporate & Editorial Office
A 63, Sector 58, Noida 201 301, U.P., India

phone: +91 120 455 3581, 455 3583
email: info@maplepress.co.in
website: www.maplepress.co.in

2018 Copyright © Maple Press Private Limited

ALL RIGHTS RESERVED. No part of this book may be reproduced or transmitted in any form by any means, electronic or mechanical, including photocopying and recording, or by any information storage and retrieval system, except as may be expressly permitted in writing by the publisher.

Printed in 2020

ISBN: 978-93-88304-14-6

Illustration by Artyfino
Printed at DD Offset Press, Noida, India

10 9 8 7 6 5 4 3 2

Contents

1.	The Ungrateful Man	4
2.	The Lion and the Carpenter	8
3.	The Fake Monk	12
4.	The Girl Who Married a Cobra	16
5.	The Role of Fate	20
6.	The Crane and the Mongoose	24
7.	The Swan and the Owl	28
8.	The Monkey and the Crocodile	32
9.	The Cobra and the Frog King	36
10.	The Lioness and the Young Jackal	40
11.	The Donkey in Tiger Skin	44
12.	The Smart Jackal	48
13.	The Unhappy Dog	52
14.	The Lion and the Foolish Donkey	54
15.	The Truthful Potter	58
16.	The Carpenter and the Camel	62
17.	The King and the Monkey	66
18.	The Three Fishes	70

The Ungrateful Man

Once there lived a poor and lazy brahmin named Yajnadatta. Tired of his nagging wife, he left his home. On the way through the forest, he heard some voices coming from a well. Peeping into it, he saw a tiger, a monkey, a snake and a man at the bottom of the well.

As soon as the tiger saw him he called out, "Sir, please help us."

The brahmin said, "No, I can't. You will eat me after I take you out." The tiger replied, "We promise that we will not harm you."

With the help of a rope he pulled them out of the well. The three animals

thanked him and said, "Please give us a chance to repay your kindness. But remember; don't trust that man in the well. He may harm you." But out of pity Yajnadatta helped the man to come out of the well too.

The man said, "I am a goldsmith. I live in the nearby town and if ever you require my help, I will be happy to help you." The brahmin continued his journey. On the way, he remembered his monkey friend. The monkey offered him lots of delicious fruits to eat. After that he reached the tiger's place.

On seeing him, the tiger was happy and gave him some jewels belonging to a prince whom he had killed. Then he met his goldsmith friend and asked, "Can you sell these jewels and get me some money?"

The moment the goldsmith saw the jewels, he recognized them as

the prince's jewels. He thought, "If I will take them to the king, I will certainly be rewarded." He said, "Wait here, I will come back soon."

He went straight to the king's palace and showed the jewels to the king. The king immediately recognized them and asked, "How did you get these jewels? He replied, "I got these jewels from a brahmin."

The king ordered to arrest the brahmin and put him in the prison. When the brahmin was put in the prison, he at once thought of the snake. The snake came and the brahmin requested the snake to help him get out of the prison. The snake said, "I will bite the queen. No medicine will cure her of my poison. I shall see to it that the touch of your hand alone will be able to cure her. Then they will release you."

The snake bit the queen and no physicians could cure her. The brahmin sent word for the king that he had a cure for the queen.

When he touched the queen, she came back to life. The brahmin then told the entire story to the king. The king imprisoned the goldsmith and rewarded the brahmin. The brahmin became rich and lived happily ever after.

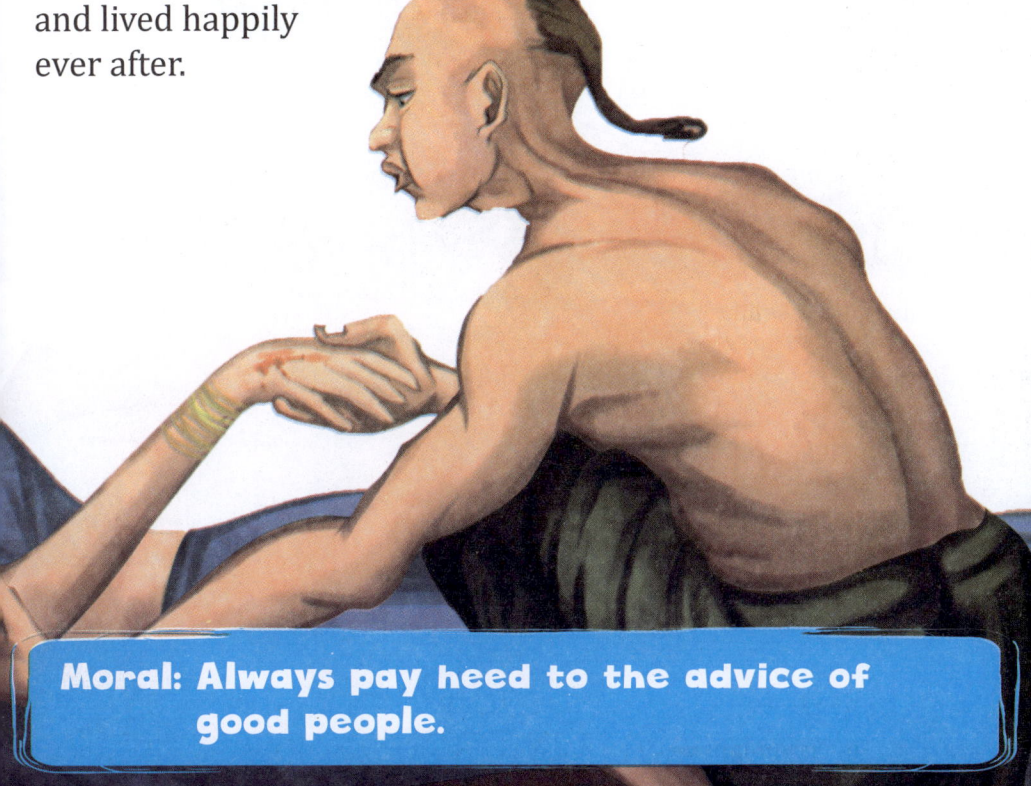

Moral: Always pay heed to the advice of good people.

The Lion and the Carpenter

One day, Daivachitha a carpenter was cutting wood in a forest when a lion came by. Seeing the lion, Daivachitha got so frightened that he thought, "Oh my god! How can I escape from this lion? I must use my wisdom."

Then he bowed to the lion and said, "Welcome my friend! Why don't you share my lunch?"

The lion roared, "You foolish man! Don't you know I'm a flesh-eating animal."

Daivachitha insisted, "My friend, I know you're a meat

eater. But just today, taste the food my wife has made."

The lion accepted his food and said, "Very delicious. I've never tasted such food in my life... My friend, I'm pleased by your hospitality. You can move freely in this forest. Neither me nor my people will harm you."

Daivachitha thanked the lion and said, "My friend, I will bring food everyday but you should come alone to meet me." The lion would go to meet his friend every day, alone.

The lion had two assisstants with whom he always shared his food. When the two friends did not get their share of food, they got impatient and decided to follow their master. They saw their master having lunch with Daivachitha.

After some time, when the lion returned to his den, the jackal went to him and said, "My lord you hunt alone these days, and we remain hungry. Please take us with you, sir."

The lion curtly replied, "Listen! I've promised my friend who brings me food everyday that I will come alone."

When the two assistants insisted the lion thought for a while and then said, "Ok! Then follow me tomorrow when I go to him."

The next day Daivachitha saw the lion coming towards him with two other animals. He thought, "I can't trust him anymore." He then climbed on to a nearby tree. When the lion requested him to come down and meet his friends he said, "You've not kept your promise. I'm not afraid of you. But I can't trust your friends."

Moral: Even a good king cannot be trusted if he has villainous advisors.

The Fake Monk

Once a king named Suradha ruled Ayodhya. He had a wise minister named Dheerbal. The king sent Dheerbal to punish a rebellious chief. One day, a fake monk came to the city and became famous for his astrological predictions. When the king heard about him, he sent his soldiers to bring the monk to him.

As soon as the fake monk came, the king bowed to him and said, "Stay with me for sometime as my guest, and be my advisor."

The monk was pleased to hear this and stayed with the king.

One day, the monk appeared before the king and said, "O king! I have good news for you. When I met Lord Indra, he enquired about your welfare."

The king was surprised and asked, "How did you meet him?"

The monk said, "I left the earthly body and assuming a heavenly body went to the heaven to meet the Gods who were eager to receive me." The foolish king believed him and started attending to all the wishes of the monk and neglected his duties.

In the meantime, Dheerbal, who was away from the city for a few months returned. He found that in his absence, the monk had been fooling the king. He thought, "If I have to save the king from the clutches of this fake monk, I must think of some plan."

He went straight to the king and said, "Oh king, I've heard a great lot about the miracles done by this monk." He then told the monk, "Show us your divine powers."

The monk said, "If you want to see my miracles put me in a cell and lock the doors. I'll go to heaven and come back safely."

Dheerbal did as he was directed. He then asked the king, "My Lord, how is it possible for the monk to go to the heaven and come back?"

The king replied, "Dheerbal, don't you know that he will leave this body in his cell and get a heavenly body to go to the heaven."

Dheerbal said, "Then I have an idea. Let us burn his earthly body. Then we can see his heavenly body forever after he returns from there."

The king got excited and said, "Splendid idea, Dheerbal!"

The cell in which the monk was locked was put on fire. This sudden and unexpected action made the monk to run away from the palace.

Thus, the king realized that he was being fooled by the monk.

Moral: You should not be carried away by falsities.

The Girl Who Married A Cobra

There once lived a Brahmin who had no children. His wife felt miserable and often cried about this.

One day, the Brahmin went to his wife with a fruit and said, "Don't weep, my dear! Today I met a sage who gave me this fruit and told me to give it to you. He said that if you eat this fruit, you will have a son in one year."

The Brahmin's wife was delighted and she took the fruit from his hand and ate it at once. After a year, to everyone's amazement she gave birth to a snake. Everyone around her advised them to get rid of the snake. But being a mother, the Brahmin's wife was very much attached to her son, the snake.

Years passed by, and the snake was fully grown. The Brahmin's wife told her husband, "See, it's time we married off our dear son... We have to get him a bride."

So the Brahmin said, "Alright, I'll try to bring a bride for our son." He then started the search of a bride for his cobra son. He travelled far and wide, and after a few months came to a friend's house.

The friend said, "Oh, my dear friend! What a surprise! I'm so happy to see you after a long time. What brings you here?"

The Brahmin said, "Dear friend, I'm in search of a beautiful bride for my son."

The friend said, "Is that the matter? Thank goodness! I've a daughter of marriageable age. Will you accept her as your daughter-in-law?"

The Brahmin was dumb-founded. He fumbled for words, "But...but... wouldn't you like to see my son first?"

The friend said, "No, no! Not at all! I know you very well, my dear friend. Is that not enough?"

The Brahmin returned to his house with the bride, and his wife said, "My son is so blessed! His bride is so beautiful."

After some time, the bride was surrounded by some bride's maids. One of them asked her, "My dear girl, have you seen the bridegroom?"

Another lady said, "The poor girl has been cheated. The bridegroom is a snake."

One more lady suggested, "now's the time! Run away quietly before it's too late!"

However the girl ignored all this saying, "No, no! I'll not leave my husband! I'll stay with him for ever. No one can change my fate."

The girl starting living with the snake and served him with all devotion.

One night, she got up from her sleep and saw a handsome man in front of her.

She was shocked, and asked him "Oh my God! Who are you?"

The man said, "Dear, don't be frightened. I'm your husband."

The girl denied, "No, it can't be possible. My husband is a snake."

So the man showed her by changing himself into a snake and getting inside the snake skin. The girl was very happy to see him. From that day onwards, every night, the cobra would become a handsome man, and in the morning would become a snake again.

The Brahmin came to know about this. He told his wife, "My dear! We must stop our son from entering the body of the snake."

The Brahmin couple waited in the night till the snake changed into the human form. Then they quietly took the snake's lifeless body and burnt it. Seeing this, the son thanked his father as he was relieved of a curse and could now stay as a man forever...

Thus the family lived happily everafter.

Moral: Unfavourable situations can sometimes be changed.

The Role of Fate

Indra, the Lord of the three worlds had a wise and intelligent parrot named Sumakamala who used to entertain all visitors coming to heaven. She was indeed the favourite of all gods. Sumakamala was a beautiful bird which had bright green feathers and a shiny red beak. She was not only intelligent and scholarly but also had many virtues to her credit. But still, pride did not overpower her qualities.

One day, Lord Indra and his courtiers were listening to Sumakamala's discourse on scriptures, when Yama, the Lord of Death came there. Seeing him, Sumakamala got frightened and took refuge in the hands of Lord Indra. Lord Indra too got worried at the arrival of Lord Yama, as his coming portends death. Lord Indra, however, asked Sumakamala, "Why do you shudder at the sight of Lord Yama?"

Sumakamala replied, "Oh Lord! I'm afraid of Yama because he always brings death. He brings sorrow to all living beings. So I feel that I should keep away from him."

Indra assured her, "But he has now simply come to see us. He won't harm you." Then he said to Yama, "O Yama! Please promise that you will spare this parrot from death. It is a humble request from all of us."

But Yama said, "How can I promise that? I have no say in this regard. I am not exactly the one who decides the death of anyone."

Indra asked in return, "Then who decides it?"

Yama said, "It's the Kalapurusha, the God of Time, who decides it."

Now the Gods decided to save the life of Sumakamala. So they went to Kalapurusha, the God of Time and said, "Oh Kalapurusha, we all have a request on behalf of this parrot."

Kalapurusha was surprised at the presence of all Gods at one time, to speak on behalf of the bird. So he asked them, "What's the matter? Why have you all come to me in unison?"

The Gods said, "We request you to spare this parrot's life."

But Kalapurusha explained to them, "No, no, I cannot save this parrot's life. I can't do anything about it. It's Mrithyu, the God of Death who decides it."

Indra and the Gods once again took the parrot and marched to Mrithyu. The moment the parrot looked at Mrithyu, she fell dead. Indra and the Gods were shocked. Lord Indra asked Yama, "Yama! What's this? Why and how did this happen? Why did the poor parrot die just at the sight of Death?"

Yama now explained, "Did I not say that the parrot's death is not in my hands? See, just by looking at Mrithyu the parrot has died."

Indra was confused. He asked Yama, "But how did this happen?"

Yama explained, "It was the rule of fate that Sumakamala should die at the sight of Mrithyu."

Having got this clear reply, the Gods and Lord Indra returned to their heavenly abode, feeling pity for the parrot.

Moral: What is prefigured must come into being.

The Crane and the Mongoose

In a forest, there was a big banyan tree where cranes lived in huge numbers. A cobra came to live inside the hollow of the tree. The cranes usually left their eggs in the nest when they went away in search of food. But, they always found their eggs missing when they returned to the tree. The reason behind this was the evil cobra.

As soon as the cranes left their eggs, he climbed up the tree and reached the nest. He would feast himself by feeding on the young cranes as soon as they came out of their eggs. This went on continuously for many days. The parent cranes were highly distressed at the loss of their young ones but were unable to understand anything. Then, one day, a mother crane finally found out that it was the cobra that was responsible for the deaths of all her babies. She felt very sad and started crying. A crab was passing by the tree. He saw the poor crane crying and asked her,

"My dear friend, you seem to be very sad. Why are you crying? What has happened to you? If you tell me your problem, I can help you."

The mother crane told the crab, "Friend, thank you so much for your concern. I am crying because I have lost all my babies. I am extremely sad to know about the way my babies

got killed. The cobra here eats away my babies when we are away searching for food. I don't know how to get rid of this cobra and save my children."

On hearing her story the crab thought, "These cranes have been our enemies since time immemorial. Why should I help them? This seems to be a good chance to take revenge on them."

Then he said to the crane, "Friend, I have

a very good idea that will help you get rid of the cobra. A mongoose lives nearby. Take some fish and pieces of meat and put them in and around the mongoose's burrow. Then make a trail of it to the cobra's home in this tree. The mongoose will follow the trail and reach the cobra's home, and then kill it."

The crane did as the crab advised her. As expected, the mongoose caught smell of the fish and meat, and then, following the trail laid by the mother crane, reached the tree. It ate the snake and reached the nest of the cranes too, and killed all of them.

Moral: A problem can be solved only by your friend and not by your enemy.

The Swan and the Owl

Once upon a time there was a swan that lived peacefully in a pond surrounded by many trees. One day, an owl came to the pond and exclaimed, "Wow! What a nice place it is. I have never seen such a beautiful place in my life!"

When the swan saw the owl watching the pond, he asked him, "Hey! Who are you? What are you doing here?"

The owl wanted to be the swan's friend and therefore he said to him, "Are you the swan that has been living in this pond since a long time? I have heard about your good nature from many other birds. I always wanted to meet you and be your friend."

The swan was pleased to hear the owl's words and said, "My friend, thank you so much for your compliment. Please be my guest. I will be happy to be your host."

Days passed by and they became very good friends. One day, the owl said to the swan, "Friend, it's been a long time since I came here as your guest. I think it is time that I part with you. Please give me your leave. You have been a great host."

The swan thanked the owl and they parted with each other.

After some days, the swan started missing his friend and thought of visiting him. He went to the tree where the owl had its nest and called out to him. On seeing the swan, the owl was extremely pleased and said, "My dear

friend! I am so happy to see you after such a long time. Please stay with me for a few days and let me serve you as my guest." The swan readily agreed to his proposal.

The swan was enjoying the hospitality of the owl when one day a group of travellers came to camp near the tree where the owl lived. When they were about to leave, the owl started hooting loudly. The travellers grew anxious and thought that a misfortune would befall them. One of them shouted, "Kill that owl immediately. It's hooting is an ill omen for us!"

Hearing him, another traveller took out his bow and aimed an arrow at the owl. But he missed his aim and accidently the arrow hit the swan. The innocent swan lost his life.

Moral: It is a grave mistake to make friends with people who are associated with evil.

The Monkey and the Crocodile

A monkey named Raktamukha, lived on a big blackberry tree situated on a river coast. One day a crocodile named Karalamukha, came out of the river looking for food, and sat under the tree.

Seeing Karalamukha, Raktamukha said, "Welcome friend, you are my guest, so please have some fruits." Saying this, the monkey threw down a lot of berries from the tree. Karalamukha found the fruits very delicious and after filling his stomach he took some of them to his home for his wife. It became a habit of Karalamukha to visit Raktamukha everyday and enjoy the fruits that he offered.

One day, Karalamukha's wife asked him, "Where do you get these fruits? They are very sweet and I have never tasted such delicious fruits in my life before."

Karalamukha replied, "A very dear friend of mine, Raktamukha gives me the fruits every day."

Immediately his wife said, "If the fruits are so sweet, the heart of your friend must also be very sweet as he eats them everyday. If you really love me, please bring his heart for me to eat."

Karalamukha, tried to convince her, "My dear, how can I kill a friend who gives me fruits every day?"

But his wife insisted, "If you really love me, you have to kill the monkey and bring me his heart. If not, I'll starve to death."

Next day Karalamukha reached the tree a bit late. Seeing him worried, Raktamukha said, "Why are you late today? What's the matter?"

"Well," replied Karalamukha, "My wife is very angry at me. She told me that I am an ungrateful friend, as I have never invited you to our home. If you do not come with me today, she will leave me and go away. So please come with me. You can sit on my back and I will carry you to my home."

Raktamukha thought for some time and then sat on Karalamukha's back. While crossing the river, Karalamukha started diving into the deep waters. The monkey got scared and told him to go slowly.

Seeing Raktamukha scared, Karalamukha said "My dear friend, I am sorry, I've fooled you! My wife wanted to eat your heart and I had no other choice but to bring you here."

With great presence of mind, Raktamukha instantly said, "Oh! My friend, why didn't you tell me before we started the journey? I have left my heart on the tree." Seeing a surprised Karalamukha, Raktamukha continued "As we jump on trees, we leave our heart on the tree so that it is safe. Let us go back and bring it."

Karalamukha believed Raktamukha's words, and as soon as they reached the banks of the river, Raktamukha jumped on to the blackberry tree.

Karalamukha waited for Raktamukha to come down with the heart. But when he did not come down Karalamukha asked, "Friend, what's delaying you? Come down quickly, my wife will be waiting for us."

Now Raktamukha laughed heartily at him, and said, "You fool! Have you seen anyone keeping his heart away? By God's grace I've got back my life. Go away from here, and never ever come back."

Moral: Never trust a wicked person.

The Cobra and the Frog King

Gangadatta, the king of frogs, lived in a well. He was not liked by his people, so he decided to leave his kingdom and left the well. He wanted to teach his people a lesson.

He noticed a cobra named Priyadarsana entering his pit. Suddenly, an idea came to him, "What if I lead this deadly cobra into my well. If will teach a lesson to my kinsmen, who made my life miserable?" The frog king stood at the entrance of the snake pit and said, "Priyadarsana, please come out."

The cobra thought, "Who could this fellow be? He does not seems to be one of us. I should not trust a stranger. So, I will stay inside until I find out who this person is? Then the cobra shouted from inside, "Who are you?"

The frog king said, "I am Gangadatta, king of frogs. I have come to seek your help."

The cobra said, "I cannot believe you. Can there be friendship between a blade of dry grass and fire?"

The frog king convinced him saying, "It is true that you are my enemy. But, now I need your help in taking revenge on my own kinsmen."

The cobra said, "How can I help you?"

The frog king said, "Come with me to the well where I live. Go inside and eat all the frogs except my family."

The snake crawled inside the well and ate all the enemies of the frog king.

Finding no more frogs to eat, the cobra told the frog king, "Friend! I have eaten all your enemies. Now I need some more frogs as I am hungry."

The frog king told him, "Now only my family is left. Please go back to your place."

The cobra protested, "How can I go back? Someone must have occupied my house now. I will stay here, and you have to provide me with food. You can offer me just a frog everyday and if you don't, then I shall eat all of them."

Hearing this threat, the frog king thought, "What a terrible mistake I have made in making an enemy as my friend! I must get out of the trap of the cobra."

The frog king started giving one frog a day to him to eat. But the cobra ate many other frogs behind his back. One by one, all the frogs in the well were eaten up, except the frog king. Now the cobra asked for more frogs.

The frog king said, "Friend, don't worry. I'm here to help you. I will bring the frogs from the other wells and offer them to you as food." Saying this it went out of the well.

The cobra, after a long wait realized that he had been fooled by the frog king. So he thought of a plan to bring him back to the well.

After a long time, the cobra addressed a lizard which also lived in the well. He said, "Please tell the frog king that he need not take the trouble of finding food for me. Let him come back to his old place. I am really missing my beloved friend."

The lizard conveyed this message to the frog king. The frog king said, "I won't go back. One terrible blunder has already landed me in trouble."

Thus, the frog king never returned to his well.

Moral: Never make friendship with an enemy.

The Lioness and the Young Jackal

Once upon a time, there lived in a forest, a lion and lioness with their newly-born cubs. Every day, the lion went out to hunt and brought food for the lioness and the cubs. The lioness stayed behind to look after the cubs. One day, the lion wandered all over the forest in search of food but could not find any prey at all. When he was returning to his home, he found a baby jackal in the forest. There was no one around him. The jackal seemed to be all alone. Thus, the lion took the baby jackal to his house.

When he reached his home, he told the lioness, "My dear! I am afraid but I was unable to get any food today, except this baby jackal that had been left by his family. Since he is still a baby, I could not bring myself to kill him. But you may do so if your hunger is uncontrollable."

The lioness got extremely angry on hearing these words of the lion and said, "No way! Do you think that I am so cruel? How can I kill a baby animal and become a sinner in the eyes of the Almighty? I shall never commit such a misdeed and take care of him like my other babies."

Thereafter, the baby jackal became a member of the lion family and they all ate, drank, played and slept together. One day when they were playing, an elephant passed by. One of the lion's cub said to the other, "Hey, look there! How dare that elephant come near our home! Let's attack him."

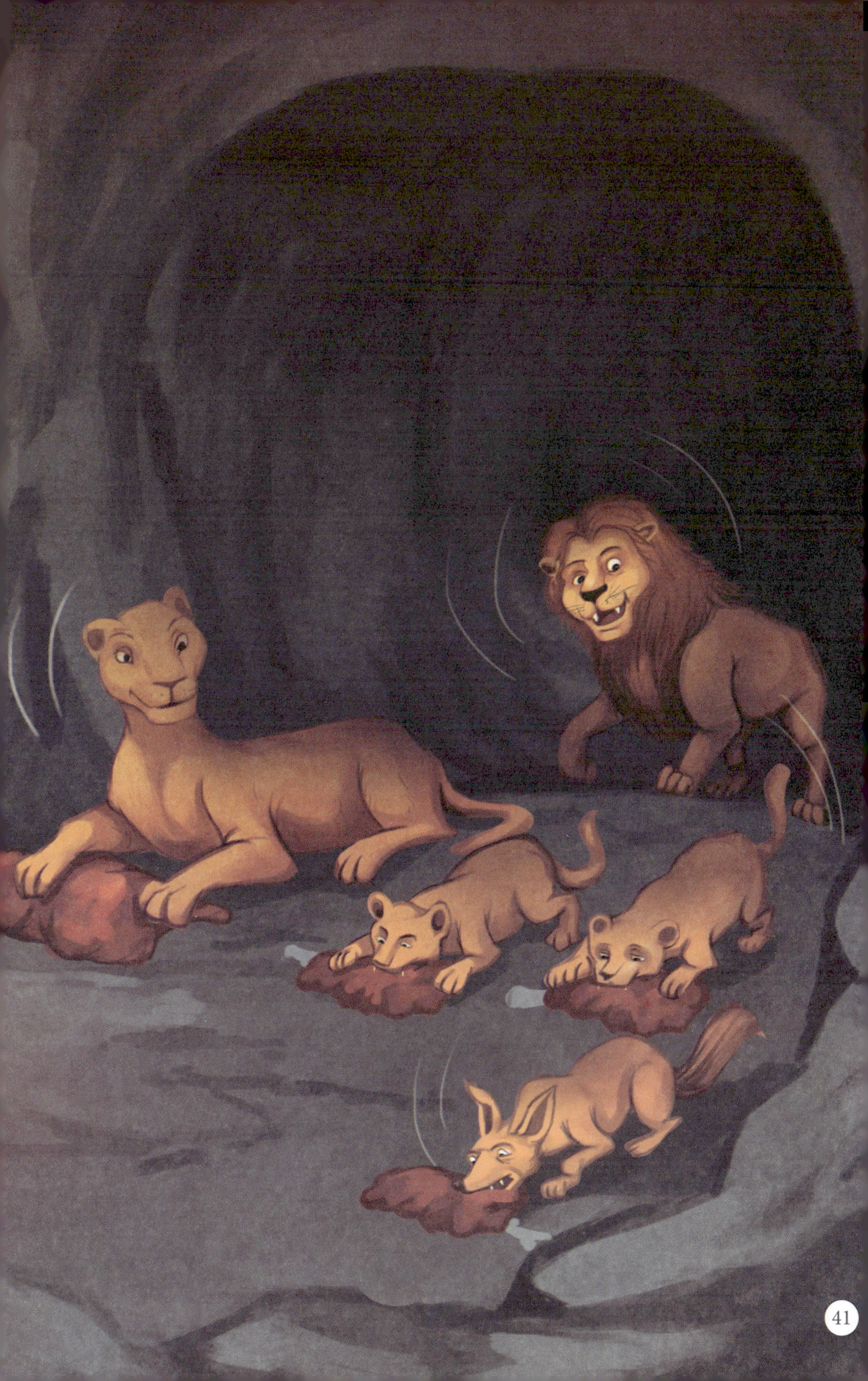

But the baby jackal stopped them saying, "No, no brothers! See how big he is; and he's so powerful that even if we attack him together we will not be able to overpower him. So it is better to run away and save our lives."

Though disappointed, the lion cubs agreed with him and all of them went back home. As soon as they entered their house, the lion cubs told the lioness, "Mother! We have something to tell you. A very funny thing happened today. We saw an elephant coming towards us. We said we would attack him, but our jackal brother got frightened by his sight and so we all ran away."

Reacting to this comment, the jackal said, "Shut up you all! Don't make me lose my temper!"

Listening to this, the lioness took the baby jackal aside and told him, "My son, don't get angry with them. They are your brothers after all!"

The jackal was hurt and asked his lion mother, "How am I inferior to them? Why do they keep ridiculing me every time? I will kill both of them if they make fun of me ever again."

Amused by the words of the baby jackal and wishing him a long life, the lioness said, "You are still a child. I brought you up taking pity on you. Your brothers are also young. Before they grow old and know that you are different from them, you should leave this place and join your own folk."

Realizing the danger he could face in future, the young jackal left the lion family in search of his own folk.

Moral: Know the truth about yourself and act accordingly.

The Donkey in Tiger Skin

Once upon a time there lived a washer-man in a village. His name was Suddhapata and he had a donkey. Suddhapata was a poor man who had a large family with a wife and seven children. He was unable to provide adequate food to the donkey and could not take proper care of him. The donkey was fed up of his hunger and prayed to God, "Oh God! Please help me! I am starving and have no energy left in my body to carry the heavy loads."

One day Suddhapata was passing through the forest. He found a tiger skin lying there and an idea stuck him - "I should cover my donkey with this skin and let him graze in the wheat fields. People will mistake him for a tiger and no one would dare to go near him. This way, my poor donkey will have plenty of food to eat!"

He went home and covered his donkey with the skin. After covering him, he told him, "Oh my dear fellow! I know that I could not feed you properly due to my limited earnings. But you need not suffer anymore. You can now go to the fields and graze till your heart's content. People will think you are a tiger. No one will dare to drive you away. But keep one thing in mind - do not bray or else the village people will recognize you and you will get a good thrashing from them!"

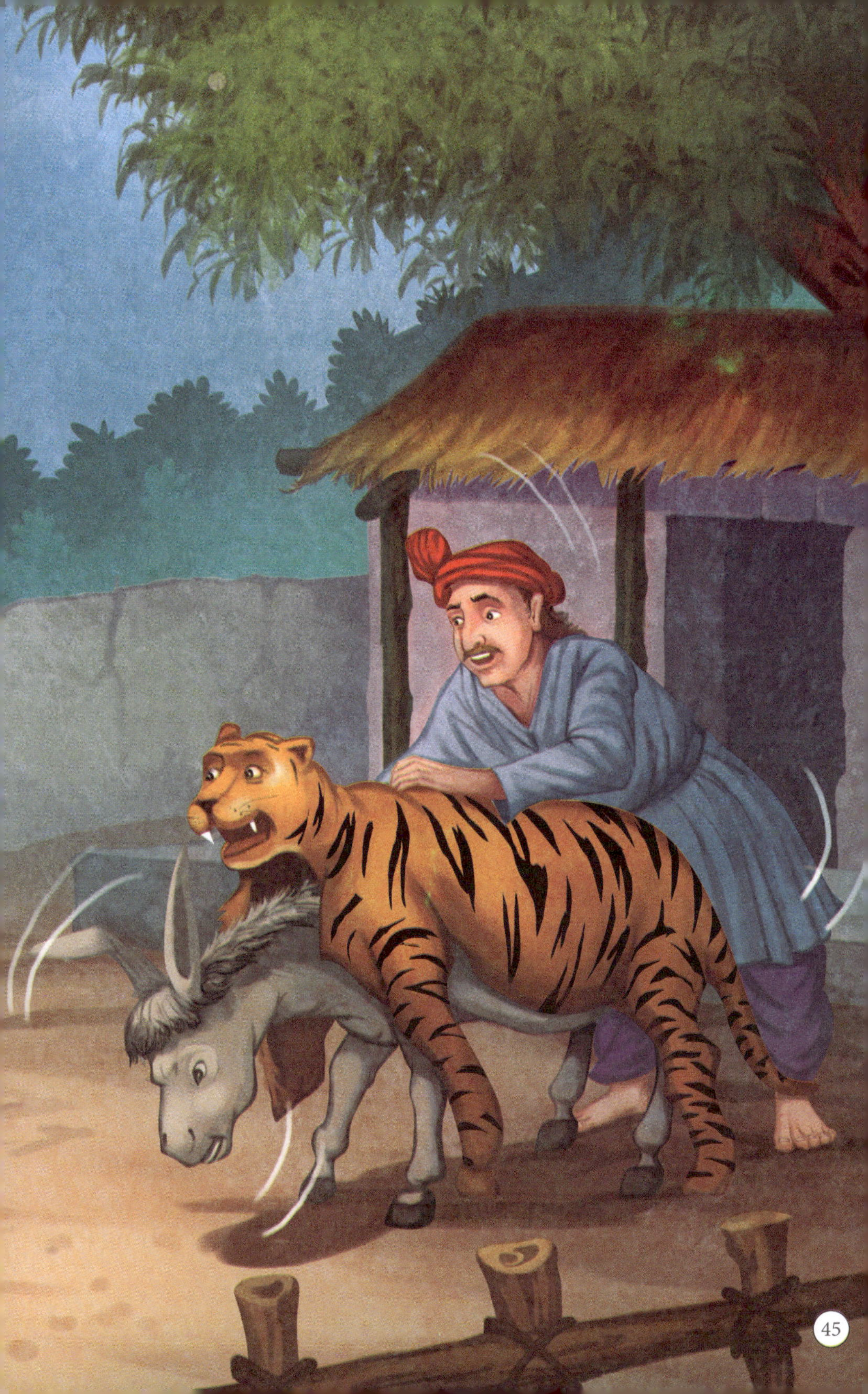

The donkey brayed in glee and began to go from one field to another and graze at leisure. People took him to be a tiger with his frightening and terrible looks and ran away as soon as they saw him, leaving the donkey alone to relish his food.

The donkey soon became fat and one day, while he was grazing, he heard the bray of another donkey, "Hooohoo... Hooohoo..."

The donkey thought, "Wow! What a charming voice! But I cannot understand whose voice it is? It must be one of my friends! It would be rude if I do not reply to the call." Thus, the donkey brayed loudly in response, "Hooohoo...Hooohoo..."

The watchman and the other people who were passing by the field heard him. At first they were confused to hear a braying voice since they could not see a donkey but rather a tiger in the field. Soon, realization dawned upon them and they recognized the donkey. They shouted out, "Oh! It's a donkey! He has been fooling us since so many days... come let's teach the fellow a good lesson..."

With these words, all of them rushed towards the donkey and started beating him. When the donkey did not return to the washerman, he went in his search from field to field. He finally found him lying dead in one of the fields and went back to his home with a heavy heart.

Moral: Silence can sometimes be golden.

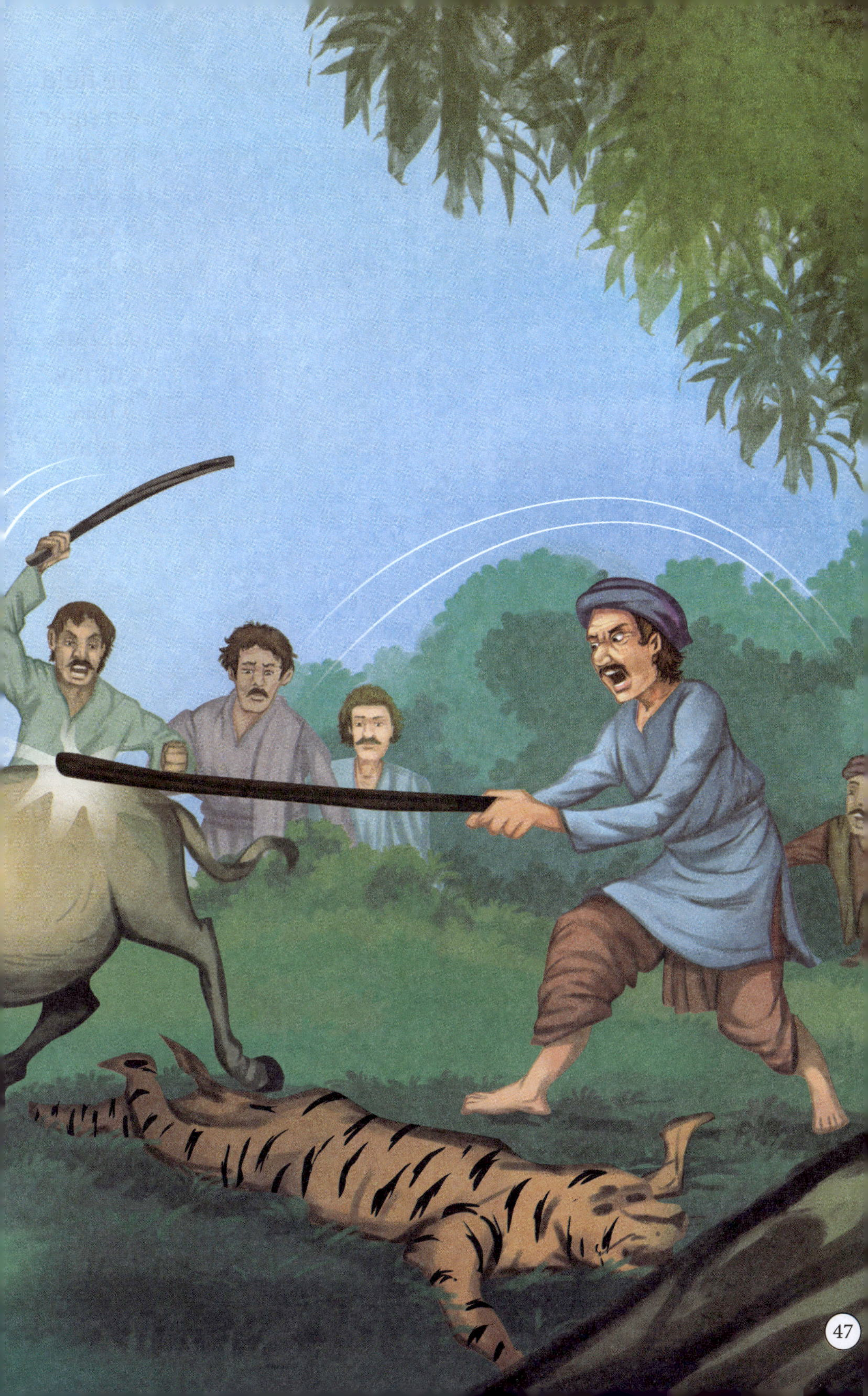

The Smart Jackal

Mahachataraka was a jackal living in a forest. One day, he found a body of an elephant and was happy that it would serve as his food for many days. However, he was not able to bite into the thick skin of the elephant and was going around the body when a lion came that way.

Mahachataraka at once started planning, and acted. He humbly prostrated before the lion and said, "Welcome, my lord! O monarch of the forest, I am your obedient servant. At your command, I am keeping a vigil on the body of the elephant. Please help yourself."

The lion said, "You know my friend, I do not eat something others have killed. You may take it as my gift to you."

"I am touched by your magnanimity, my lord," said the jackal.

After the lion had left, a tiger came on the scene. Mahachataraka thought, "I got rid of one menace through humility. How do I escape this fellow? He will not yield

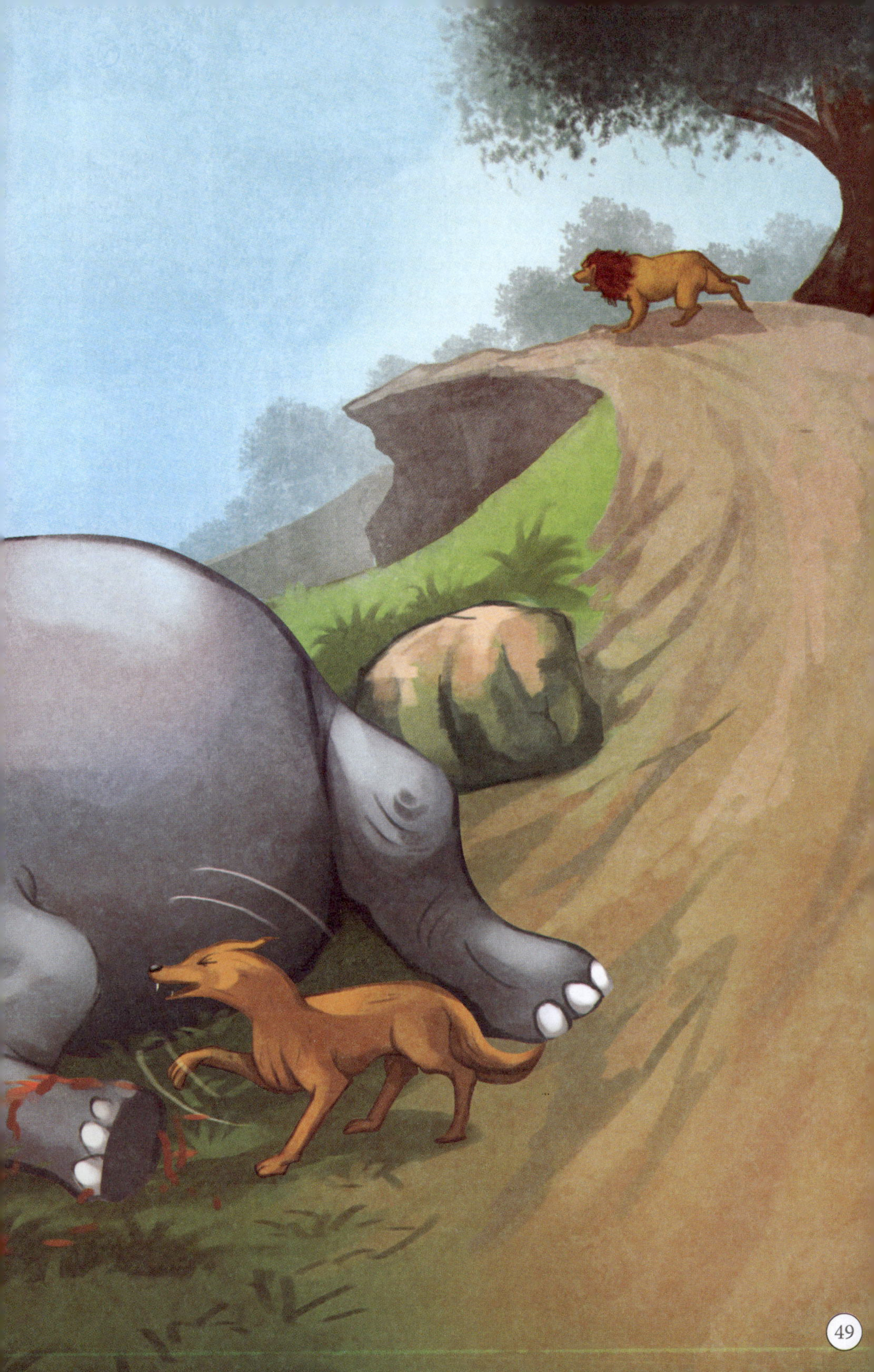

to any strategy I know. The only way of keeping him away is by a clever trick! Let me try it."

Mahachataraka then went half way to greet the tiger and said, "O sir! why are you entering this area? The lion has asked me to keep watch on the elephant. He has gone to take bath. Before going, he told me to inform him as soon as any tiger happened to come here. Please go away! You're risking your life!"

These words frightened the tiger. He told Mahachataraka, "No... no! for mercy's sake! Don't call the lion. I'll run away!"

With these words, the tiger ran away.

After some time, a leopard came by... and Mahachataraka thought, "Oh! Here's another intruder! But his sharp teeth can tear through the elephant skin for me... I should use him..."

Then Mahachataraka went to the leopard and said with a gleam, "Welcome, dear friend, to a hearty meal! A lion killed this elephant, and has gone away to take bath. Let's have this meal before he returns."

The leopard however said, "I'm pleased by your hospitality. Let me start, but alert me when the lion comes…"

As he started tearing the elephant's skin, Mahachataraka said in a panic, "O my god! The lion is coming… come on, run away fast, to save your life…"

The leopard immediately left his food, and ran away into the forest. Thus clever Mahachataraka duped the leopard and sent him away. He had just started to taste the meat, when another jackal came that way. Now, Mahachataraka thought "He's my kinsman. I know his strength, so I can fight him off." Then he attacked the other jackal and drove him away, after which he continued his meal.

Moral: It's smart to fight out with an equal.

The Unhappy Dog

Once a dog named Chitranga lived in a village. There came a year in the village when there was no rainfall in the season and that resulted into a famine. Due to this famine, the food became scarce. The dogs and other animals started dying due to hunger and their families started becoming extinct. So Chitranga decided to leave the village and go to some other town.

In the new town, he found a wealthy man's house. The woman of the house was lazy and careless, and never bothered to close the doors of her house.

Every day, Chitranga would sneak into the open house, steal the food and eat to his heart's content.

One day, when he was coming out of the house after his meal, the street dogs attacked him and wounded him severely. He was unable to even lift his body. He suddenly remembered his friends and family in the village and thought- "I think I made a mistake by coming here. Home was better even if there was no food. There was no struggle for life at least. Nobody came and fought with you like this. I must get back to my home."

Thus, he left that city and returned home. Seeing him back, his kinsmen and friends became very happy.

Moral: One may feel threatened in unknown places.

The Lion and the Foolish Donkey

A lion named Karalakesara lived in a forest. He had a faithful servant named Dhoomra, a jackal. One day, the lion was badly wounded in a fight with an elephant. He could not go out for hunting for few days after that. As a result, the jackal also had to remain without food. Both the master and the servant became very weak. Unable to bear the hunger, Dhoomra told his master Karalakesara, "Master, for over two days we've had no food. I'm starving. Please do something."

Karalakesara said, "Dhoomra! Can't you see how helpless I am. If you can go and catch some animal for me, I will give you a portion to eat."

So Dhoomra went off in search of a victim. After some time, he found a donkey Lambakarna grazing in the jungle. Dhoomra went to him and said, "O my friend! Is something wrong with you? You're looking weak and lean!"

Lambakarna said, "Oh, yes, I'm. My master has been ill-treating me. He makes me carry heavy loads, and I don't even get a proper meal after the hard work."

Dhoomra said, "What a pity! Why don't you come with me then? I will take you to a beautiful place where you can have fresh green grass and sweet water to drink. You can happily spend your time there."

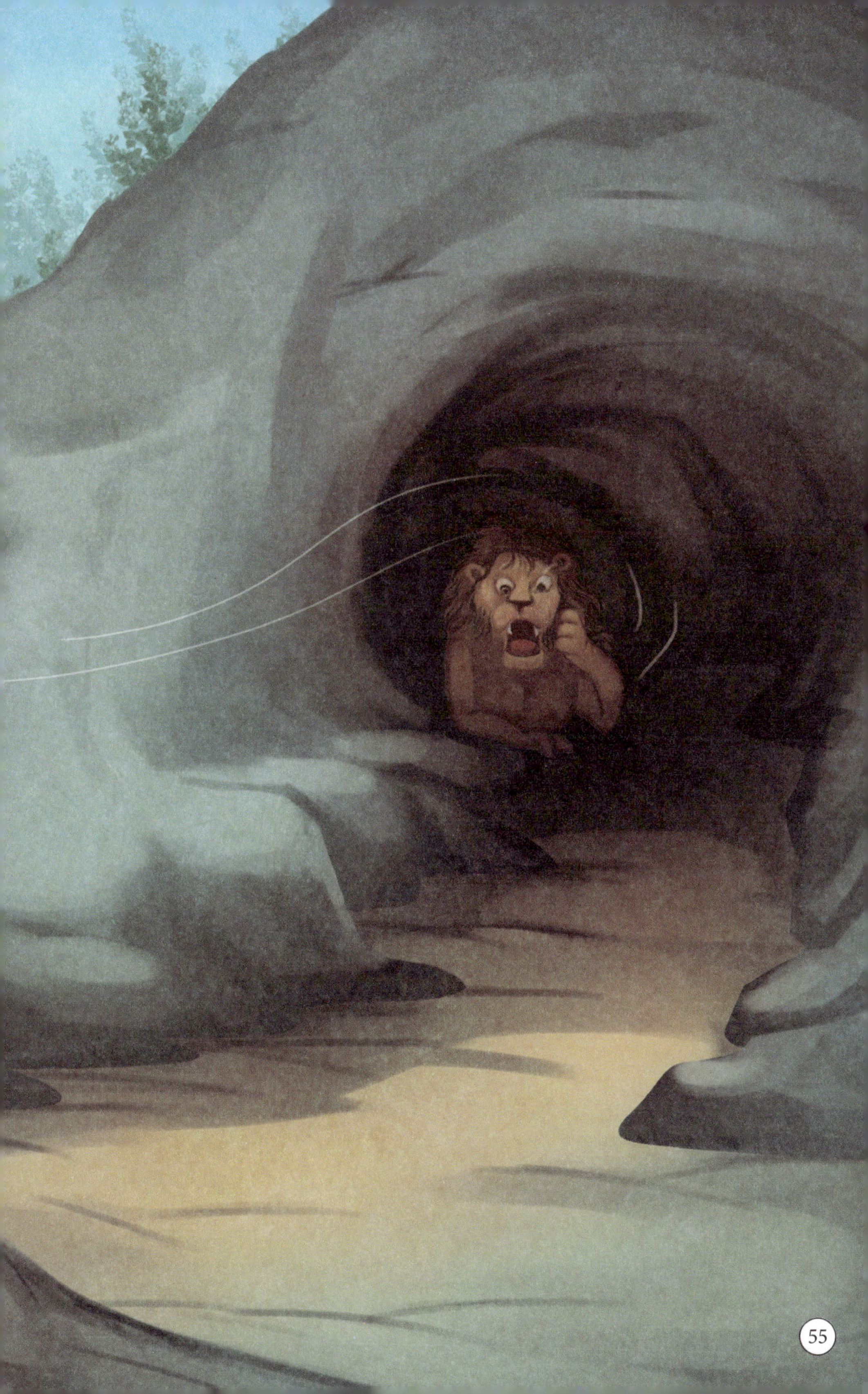

Pleased by the offer, Lambakarna agreed to go with Dhoomra, who took him to Karalakesara's den. As soon as Karalakesara the lion, saw Lambakarna, he jumped on him, but missed his aim. Lambakarna was shocked at this sudden attack and ran away at a great speed. Karalakesara made great efforts to reach him and strike him, but failed.

Angry at Karalakesara's failure, Dhoomra told him, "Sir, you've spoiled my plan. Why were you so hasty?"

Karalakesara explained, "I was so hungry that I could not control myself on seeing my prey."

Dhoomra now told, "Ok, I'll now go and try to bring him back again. But be careful not to mess up this time."

Then he went in search of Lambakarna who was now on a river bank feeding on grass. Lambakarna looked at him and asked, "Why have you come again? I'm really frightened. Who was your friend who almost killed me?"

Dhoomra said, "Oh my friend! You are so innocent. It was a female donkey, who fell in love with you the moment she saw you. She has sent a message to you that she will die if you do not return to her."

Foolish Lambakarna believed in Dhoomra's words, and followed him. Karalakesara, who was waiting for him, pounced upon him and killed Lambakarna instantly.

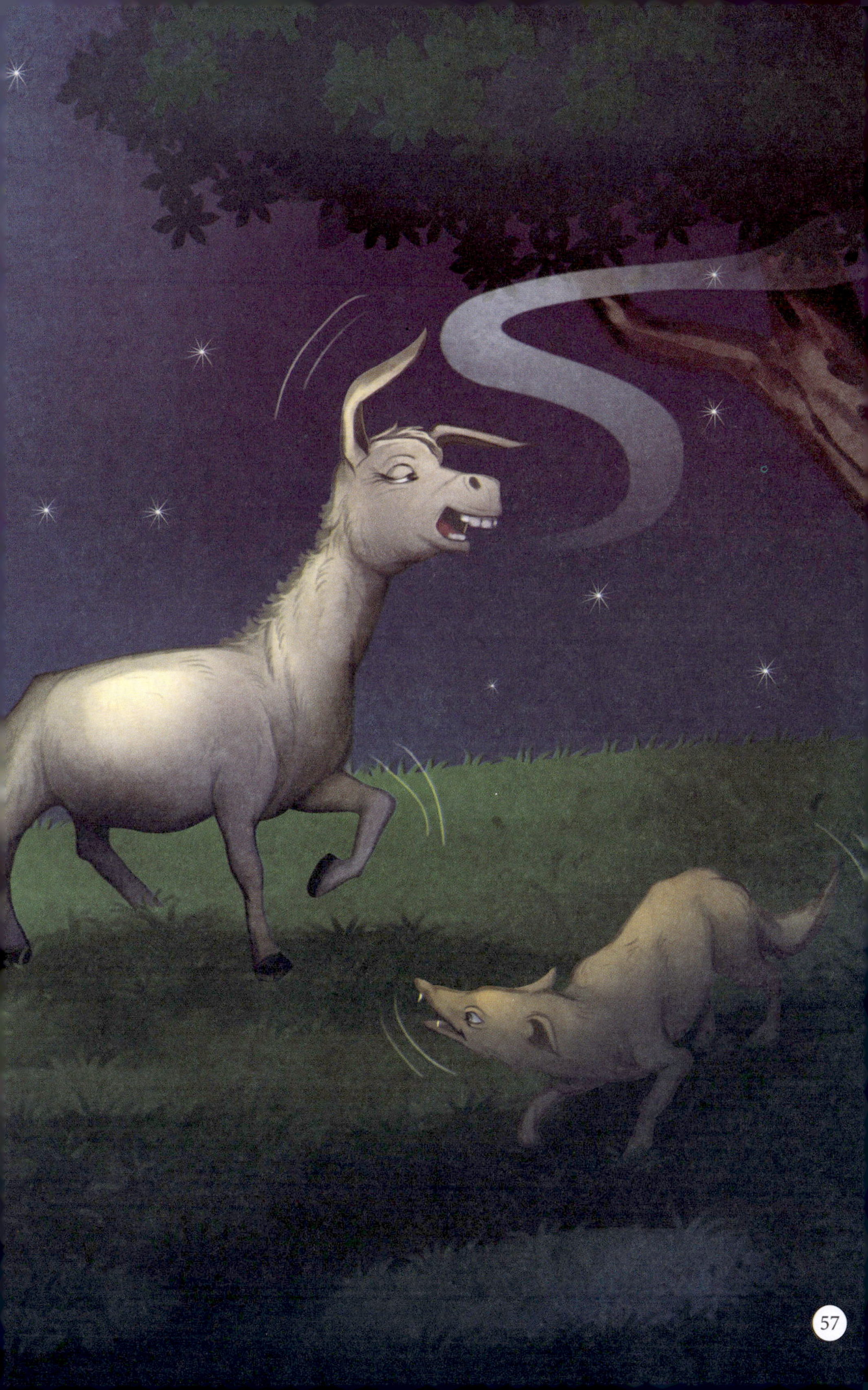

The Truthful Potter

A potter named Samaradheera lived in a village. He would make beautiful pots of various sizes and shapes and sell them in the village market in order to earn his living. One day, while carrying the pots, he lost his balance and fell on a hard surface. Unfortunately, all the mud pots broke into pieces and their sharp edges cut his forehead and cheek. He was badly hurt but somehow he managed to reach his home. He did not go to a doctor but just waited for the wounds to get healed. The pain subsided after some time but the scars of the wound remained forever on his face.

Due to scarcity of water, a severe famine struck the village. The potter was left with no other option but to leave the village. He went to a distant land with the other people, where he joined the king's army. One day, the king noticed the scars on his face and thought, "Hmm... this fellow must be a great warrior, as he has got such terrible wounds on his face..." He called his commander and told him, "Look at the scars on his face. He is a great warrior. Treat him with respect and great attention. We're lucky to have such a hero in our army!"

Soon, Samaradheera became the king's favourite and started receiving a royal treatment. Everything was going on smoothly,

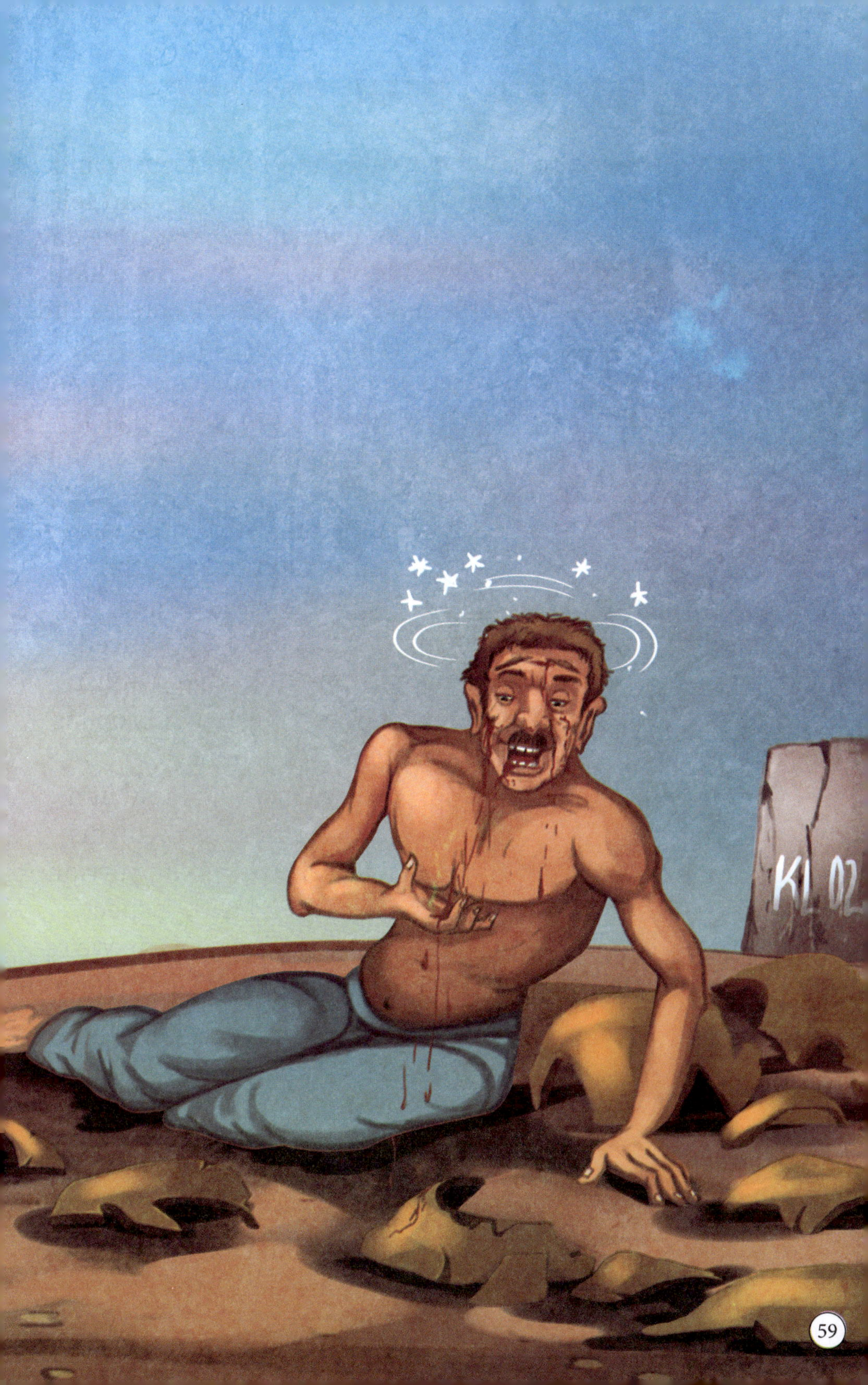
KL 02

when suddenly the enemy of the land threatened to attack the capital. The country started preparing its army for a counter attack. One day, the king came to inspect the army, and his eyes fell on Samaradheera. He called out to him "O great warrior! Tell me where and in which battle you got wounded?"

Samaradheera realised that now the time had come for him to reveal the truth. He said, "O mighty king! This is not a scar from any battle. I'm a potter and one day when I was going home with my pots, I fell down and the pieces of the broken pots pierced my face and gave me these scars."

Hearing to his confession, the king got furious. He felt that he had been deceived by the potter. He called his sentries and said, "Take this fellow away! Give him a good thrashing for his deception!"

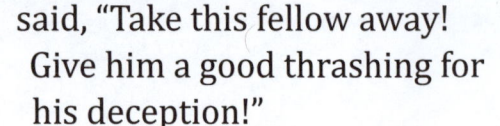

Samaradheera fell at the feet of the king and pleaded, "Your majesty! Please give me a chance! I will fight in the upcoming battle and show my valour."

But the king refused to hear anything and said, "No, no! You're a cheat. I don't want to hear you anymore. Leave this place before others come to know that you're just a potter."

Moral: Right knowledge is required to succeed.

The Carpenter and the Camel

In the city of Nagara, there was a carpenter named Ujjwalaka, who was extremely poor. He realized that every one else in his profession was rich and happy and that he alone was very poor. This thought made him very unhappy and he thought Nagara was not the proper place for him to prosper. He decided to go out and seek his fortune elsewhere. He left that city and began his journey to a new country. It was dusk when he reached a cave in a forest.

There he saw a female camel that had been separated from her caravan and had just delivered a child. Seeing them, Ujjwalaka gave up his plans to go to another country and went back to his home taking the camel and her calf with him. Every day he would go into the forest and bring back with him bundles of tender leaves for the camel and her child to eat. The camel regained her strength and the calf now became an adult. The carpenter started selling camel milk and was able get good money.

Ujjwalaka loved the camel so much that he bought a bell and hung it around her neck. One day he thought to himself, "If one camel can bring so much money for me, how much more would I earn if I buy more camels and sell their milk?" He told his wife that he would borrow some

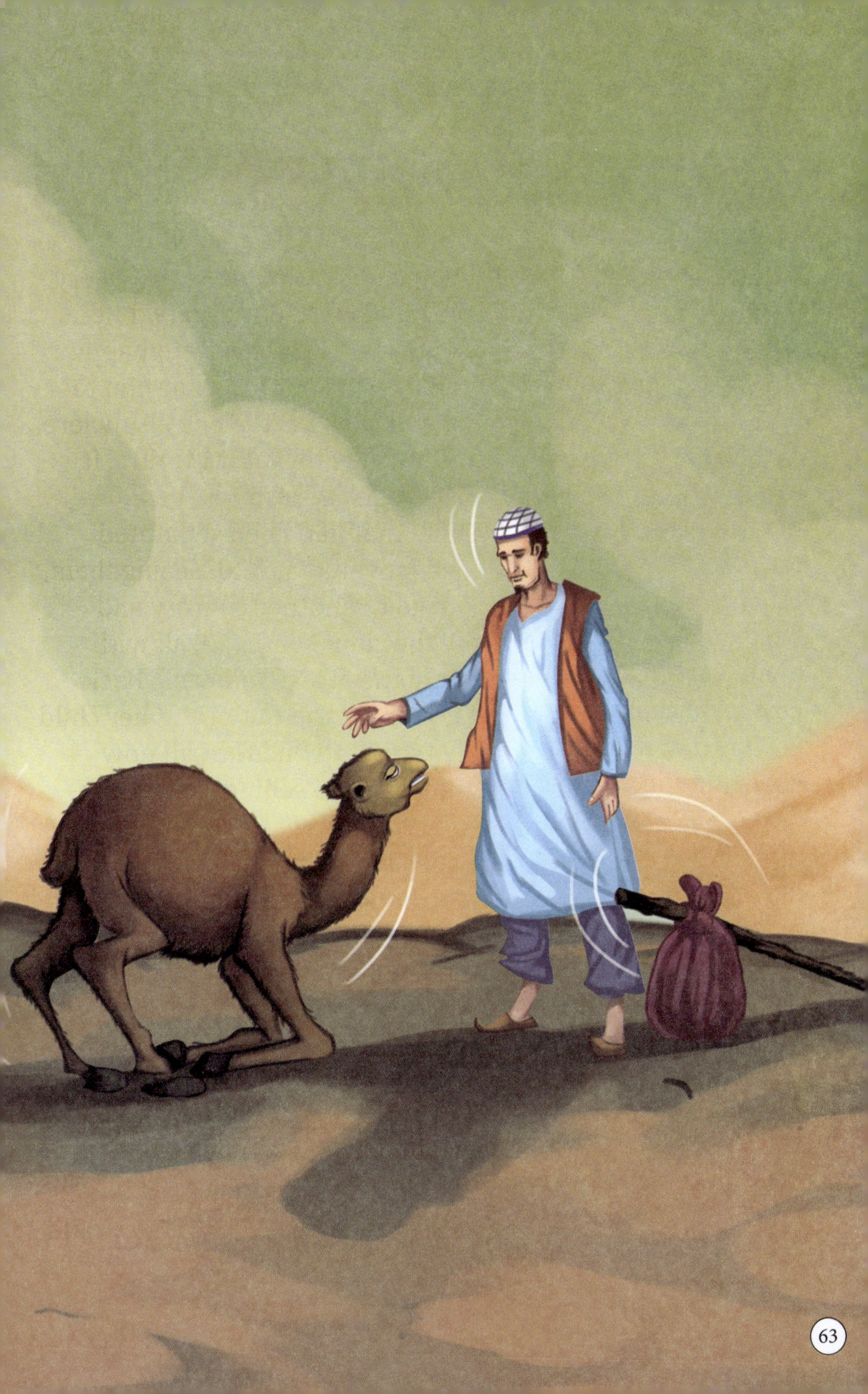

money, go to the city and buy a she camel. Until his return, he told his wife to take care of the camel and her calf.

He went to the city, got a new she camel, and returned home. Slowly, the number of camels multiplied. He appointed a caretaker to handle the camel herd on the condition that he would give one camel to the keeper every year as remuneration. The keeper was also free to drink camel milk twice a day. Now, everything was fine for the carpenter and he and his wife thus lived happily now.

The camels used to go every day to a nearby forest to feed on the fresh green leaves available in plenty in the forest. After spending a lot of time in the forest, eating and playing, the camels trekked back home. But the young camel stayed in the forest for some more time and joined the herd later. The other camels advised her to return with the herd as she might become easy prey for the animals in the jungle if she stayed alone for longer periods. They tried to convince her, but the camel was stubborn.

One day, a lion saw all the camels leaving the forest in a herd and the young camel staying back and eating the grass with leisure. By the time she finished her leisurely grazing, the others had left and reached home. The young camel lost her way and was panic-stricken to see the lion that was following her. He pounced on her soon.

Moral: Overconfidence in the most danger form of carelessness.

THE KING AND THE MONKEY

Once upon a time, there was a king, who had a pet monkey. The monkey was allowed to enter anywhere inside the palace, even where other ministers were forbidden to enter. The monkey was not only his pet but served the king as his personal servant.

The ministers of the king felt that the king was giving undue attention to the animal. They went to the king when he was alone and said, "O mighty lord! Do you know what you're doing by keeping the monkey as your pet? By giving him privilege, you're dooming yourself. A monkey is after all a monkey. He cannot take the place of a wise and sincere servant... One day or other he will prove to be a danger to you!"

The king instead of thinking over this advice of the ministers, got angry and immediately ordered their suspension. He then made the monkey his chief advisor.

Days went by, and the king was happy to have the monkey as his chief advisor. No person dared to come to near the king when the monkey was around. The royal priest, the other ministers, and even the royal security guards kept away from the king when he was alone with the monkey.

One afternoon the king had just finished eating

a heavy lunch. It was very hot outside, and thus, the king retired to his chamber. As always, the monkey followed him to his bedroom. As he lay on the bed, he told the monkey, "Look here, I am very tired. I am going to take rest. Don't allow anyone to disturb me when I am asleep."

So there was no one around, except the king and his pet monkey. The monkey started fanning the king with a hand fan. Suddenly, a fly landed on the king's bed. It flew here and there and finally sat on the king.

The monkey saw the fly sit on

the forehead of the king and tried to push it away. The fly flew away for a moment but come back again. This went on for quite some time and the monkey was now getting irritated. He thought, "How dare this fly disturb my master? Let me teach him a lesson."

He looked around and found a dagger lying near the king. He saw the fly sitting by the king's side. He took the dagger in his hand and pushed it down with all force on the fly. In the first attempt the fly flew away but after some time, it came again and sat on the king's nose. This time the monkey took a precise aim at the fly. But it again missed it. Then the fly sat on the stomach of the king, and the monkey aimed at the fly yet again. Alas! the fly missed the blow and flew away with a whiff, while the blow from the dagger fell on the king's stomach. The king immediately died, leaving the monkey to wonder about his act.

Moral: You should not have a fool as a servant.

The Three Fishes

Once upon a time, there lived in a pond three fish friends. Two of them were very hardworking and practical in their approach to living, whereas the third believed more in fate and had a laid back approach to life.

One evening, two fishermen were passing by the pond. One of them observed it carefully and said to the other, "Hey friend! Look there. This pond is so big. It must be full of fishes. We will get all the fish that we want through this pond. It will solve all our problems. Let us come here tomorrow morning with our nets and try our luck." The other one readily agreed to him and they both went away.

The two fish friends heard the fishermen talk and panicked. They went to the other fishes in the pond and told them, "Hey friends! Listen to us. We are in a great danger. We have heard the conversation of two fishermen who plan to come tomorrow and cast their nets in the pond to catch all of us. We urgently need to make an action plan. We should leave this pond at the earliest and ensure our safety."

To this, the other fish replied, "Hey! I have an idea. We do not

71

need to leave the pond. Since the pond is so big, we all can go to the other end of it and hide ourselves from the fishermen's view."

After hearing them, their third friend laughed and said, "You are cowards! Why should we go away and hide in shame? We've been living here since a long time. So far, none of our friends have been fished out by anyone. Then why are you getting afraid of these fishermen unnecessarily? If it would be in our fate to die, nobody could save us. And if not, nobody could catch us. So I don't agree with you that moving to another place will save us. I am going to stay here only and not follow you."

The two wise friends however, were well aware of the motives of the fishermen. They quickly swam to the other side of the pond with the other fishes. The next morning, the two fishermen came to the pond as planned and cast their nets.

The wise fishes got saved as the fisherman did not come to this end of the pond. The poor third friend, along with many other fishes who believed in luck were unfortunately caught in the net. Thus, it turned out to be a lucky day for the fishermen.

Moral: Those who leave things to fate and believe in luck destroy themselves.